Walter Crane, W. J. (William James) Linton, Edmund Evans

The baby's own Aesop

Being the fables condensed in rhyme

Walter Crane, W. J. (William James) Linton, Edmund Evans

The baby's own Aesop
Being the fables condensed in rhyme

ISBN/EAN: 9783741179334

Manufactured in Europe, USA, Canada, Australia, Japa

Cover: Foto ©Andreas Hilbeck / pixelio.de

Manufactured and distributed by brebook publishing software
(www.brebook.com)

Walter Crane, W. J. (William James) Linton, Edmund Evans

The baby's own Aesop

BABY'S
OWN
ÆSOP

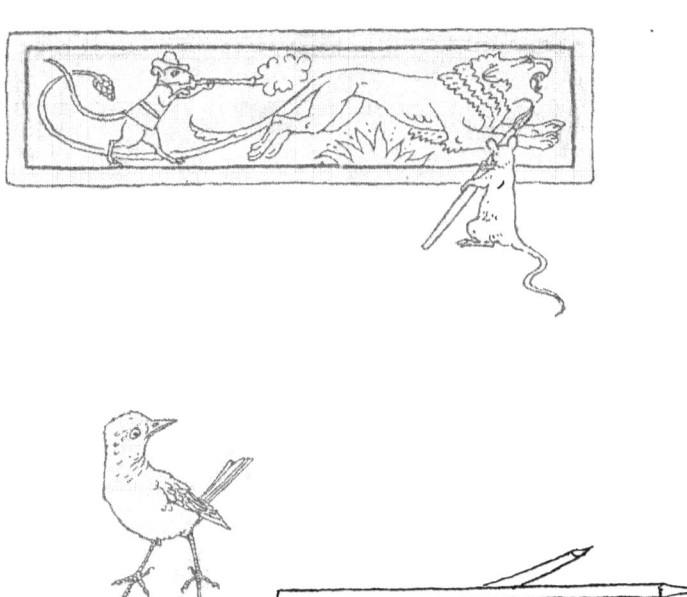

THE

BABY'S OWN ÆSOP

·BEING·THE·FABLES·CONDENSED·IN·RHYME·
·WITH·PORTABLE·MORALS·
·PICTORIALLY·POINTED·
BY

·WALTER·CRANE·

ENGRAVED & PRINTED IN COLOURS BY

EDMUND·EVANS

LONDON·& NEW YORK
GEORGE·ROUTLEDGE
& SONS
MDCCCLXXXVII

ENGRAVER & PRINTER

PREFACE

FOR this rhymed version of the Fables I have to thank my early friend and master W. J. LINTON, who kindly placed the M.S. at my disposal. I have added a touch here and there, but the credit of this part of the book still belongs to him.

Walter Crane

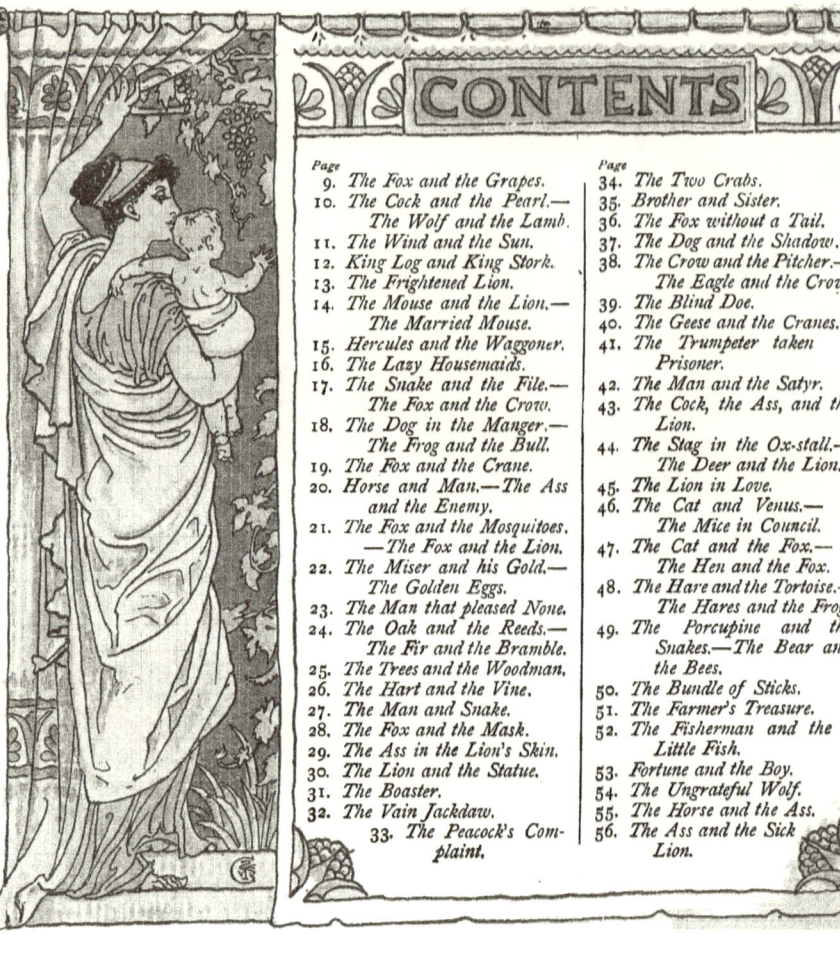

CONTENTS

ERRATA AND ADDENDA.
(CONTENTS PAGE).

Page 42.—*For* " *The Man and the Satyr*," *read Hot and Cold.*

Page 43.—*For* " *The Cock*," *&c.*, *read Neither Beast nor Bird.*

Page 52.—*For* " *The Fisherman*," *&c.*, *read* { *Cock, Ass, and Lion.* / *The Ass and the Lap Dog.*

Page 54.—*Add Fisherman and Fish.*

Page 55.—*Add The Herdsman's Vows.*

THE FOX & THE GRAPES

THIS Fox has a longing
for grapes;
He jumps, but the bunch still
escapes.
So he goes away sour;
And, 'tis said, to this hour
Declares that he's no taste
for grapes.

"THE GRAPES OF DISAPPOINTMENT ARE ALWAYS SOUR"

B

THE·COCK·&·THE·PEARL

A ROOSTER, while scratching
for grain,
Found a Pearl. He just paused to
explain
That a jewel's no good
To a fowl wanting food,
And then kicked it aside with
disdain.

"IF·HE·ASK·BREAD·WILL·YE·GIVE·HIM·A·STONE?"

THE·WOLF·AND·THE·LAMB·

A WOLF, wanting lamb for his
dinner,
Growled out—"Lamb you wronged me,
you sinner:"
Bleated Lamb—"Nay, not true!"
Answered Wolf—"Then 'twas Ewe—
Ewe or lamb, you will serve for my
dinner."

··FRAUD·AND·VIOLENCE·HAVE·NO·SCRUPLES·

THE·WIND & THE·SUN

THE WIND and the Sun had a bet,
The wayfarers' cloak which should get:
Blew the Wind – the cloak clung:
Shone the Sun – the cloak flung
Showed the Sun had the best of it yet.

·TRUE·STRENGTH·IS·NOT·BLUSTER·

KING·LOG·&·KING·STORK·

THE FROGS prayed to
Jove for a king:
"Not a log, but a livelier
thing."

Jove sent them a Stork,
Who did royal work,
For he gobbled them up, did
their king.

DON'T·HAVE·KINGS

THE FRIGHTENED LION

A BULL FROG, according
to rule,
Sat a-croak in his
usual pool:
And he laughed in his heart
As a Lion did start
In a fright from the brink
like a fool.

'IMAGINARY FEARS ARE THE WORST'

THE · MOUSE · & · THE · LION

A POOR thing the Mouse
was, and yet,
When the Lion got
caught in a net,
All his strength was no use
'Twas the poor little Mouse
Who nibbled him out of the
net.

· SMALL · CAUSES · MAY · PRODUCE · GREAT · RESULTS

THE · MARRIED · MOUSE

SO the Mouse had Miss
Lion for bride;
Very great was his joy and
his pride:
But it chanced that she put
On her husband her foot,
And the weight was too much,
So he died

· ONE · MAY · BE · TOO · AMBITIOUS ·

HERCULES & THE WAGGONER

WHEN the God saw the
Waggoner kneel,
Crying, "Hercules! Lift me
my wheel „
From the mud, where 'tis stuck!
He laughed—"No such luck;
Set your shoulder yourself
to the wheel."

·THE·GODS·HELP·THOSE·WHO·HELP·THEMSELVES·

15

THE·LAZY·HOUSEMAIDS

TWO Maids killed the
Rooster whose warning
Awoke them too soon every
morning:
But small were their gains,
For their Mistress took pains
To rouse them herself without
warning.

·LAZINESS·IS·ITS·OWN·PUNISHMENT

16

❦ THE · SNAKE · & · THE · FILE

A SNAKE, in a fix, tried
a File
For a dinner. "'Tis-not worth
your while,"
Said the steel, "don't mistake;
I'm accustomed to take;
To give's not the way of
a File."

WE · MAY · MEET · OUR · MATCH·

THE · FOX · & · THE · CROW ❦

SAID sly Fox to the Crow
with the cheese,
"Let me hear your sweet voice,
now, do please!"
And this Crow, being weak,
Cawed the bit from her beak.
"Music charms", said the Fox,
"and here's cheese!"

: BEWARE · OF · FLATTERERS :

17

THE·DOG·IN·THE·MANGER·

A COW sought a mouth=
:ful of hay;
But a Dog in the man=
=ger there lay,
And he snapped out "how now!"
When most mildly, the Cow
Adventured a morsel to pray.

· DON'T · BE · SELFISH ·

THE·FROG·&·THE·BULL·

SAID the Frog, quite puffed
up to the eyes,
"Was this Bull about me
as to size?"
"Rather bigger, frog-brother."
"Puff, puff," said the other,
"A Frog is a Bull if he
tries!"

· BRAG · IS · NOT · ALWAYS · BELIEF ·

·THE·FOX·&·THE·CRANE·

You have heard how Sir
Fox treated Crane:
With soup in a plate. When again
They dined, a long bottle
Just suited Crane's throttle;
And Sir Fox licked the outside
in vain.

·THERE·ARE·GAMES·THAT·TWO·CAN
PLAY·AT·

19

:HORSE AND MAN:

WHEN the Horse first
took Man on his back,
To help him the Stag to attack;
How little his dread,
As the enemy fled,
Man would make him his
slave & his hack.

· ADVANTAGES · MAY · BE · DEARLY · BOUGHT :

THE ASS & THE ENEMY:

"GET up! let us flee from
the Foe,"
Said the Man: but the Ass
said "Why so?"
"Will they double my load,
Or my blows? Then, by goad,
And by stirrup, I've no cause
to go."

: YOUR· REASONS· ARE·
· NOT· MINE :

THE FOX & THE MOSQUITOES

BEING plagued with Mosquitoes
one day
Said old Fox " pray don't send
them away,
For a hungrier swarm
Would work me more harm;"
I had rather the full ones
should stay."

· THERE · WERE · POLITICIANS · IN · ÆSOP'S · TIME ·

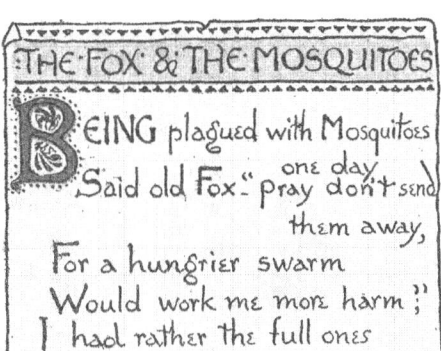

THE · FOX · & · THE · LION

THE first time the Fox
had a sight
Of the Lion, he 'most died
of fright;
When he next met his eye,
Fox felt just a bit shy;
But the next_ quite at ease,
& polite.

· FAMILIARITY · DESTROYS · FEAR · .

21

THE MISER & HIS GOLD

HE buried his Gold in a hole.
One saw, and the treasure
  he stole.
Said another, "What matter?
Don't raise such a clatter,
You can still go & sit by
          The hole."

USE · ALONE · GIVES · VALUE ·

THE · GOLDEN · EGGS

A GOLDEN egg, one every
              day,
  That simpleton's Goose
        used to lay;
So he killed the poor thing,
Swifter fortune to bring,
And dined off his fortune
        that day.

: GREED · OVEREACHES ITSELF ⌒⌒

22

THE MAN THAT PLEASED NONE

THROUGH the town
this good Man & his Son
Strove to ride as to please every one:
Self, Son, or both tried,
Then the Ass had a ride;
While the world, at their efforts,
poked fun.

YOU·CANNOT·HOPE·TO·PLEASE·ALL·"·DON'T·TRY·

THE·OAK·&·THE·REEDS·

GIANT Oak, in his
strength & his scorn
Of the winds, by the roots
was uptorn:
But slim Reeds at his side
The fierce gale did outride,
Since, by bending the burden
was borne.

:BEND, NOT·BREAK:

THE·FIR·&·THE·BRAMBLE·

THE Fir-tree looked down
on the Bramble.
"Poor thing, only able to scramble
About on the ground."
Just then an 'axe' sound
Made the Fir wish himself
but a Bramble.

·PRIDE·OF·PLACE·HAS·ITS·DISADVANTAGES·

THE · TREES & THE
· WOODMAN ·

HE TREES ask of Man
what he lacks;
"One bit, just to handle my axe?"
All he asks — well and good:
But he cuts down the wood,
So well does he handle his axe!

"GIVE · ME · AN · INCH · & · I'LL · TAKE · AN
· ELL ·"

THE·HART·&·THE·VINE·

A Hart by the hunters pur:sued,
Safely hid in a Vine, till
he chewed
The sweet tender green,
And, through shaking leaves seen,
He was slain by his ingratitude.

SPARE·YOUR·BENEFACTORS·

THE · MAN · & · THE · SNAKE ·

IN pity he brought the poor
         Snake
To be warmed at his fire.
              A mistake!
For the ungrateful thing
Wife & children would sting.
I have known some as bad as
         the Snake.

· BEWARE · HOW · YOU ·

· ENTERTAIN · TRAITORS ·

∘THE∘FOX∘&∘THE∘MASK∘

A Fox with his
foot on a
Mask,
Thus took the fair semblance
To task;
"You're a real handsome face;
But what part of your case
Are your brains in,
good Sir! let me
ask?"

∘MASKS∘ARE∘THE∘FACES∘OF∘SHAMS∘

28

"THE ASS IN THE LION'S SKIN"

WHAT pranks I
shall play!" thought
the Ass,
In this skin for a Lion to pass;"
But he left one ear out,
And a hiding, no doubt,
Lion" had – on the skin of
an Ass!

· IMPOSTORS ·
GENERALLY · FORGET ·
· SOMETHING ·

29

:THE·LION·&·THE·STATVE:

ON a Statue - King Lion
                      dethroned,
  Showing conqueror Man,—
              Lion frowned.
" If a Lion, you know,
   Had been sculptor, he'd show
Lion rampant, and Man on the
                      ground."

THE·STORY·DEPENDS·ON·THE·TELLER·

·THE·BOASTER·

IN the house, in the market, the streets,
Everywhere he was boasting his feats;
  Till one said, with a sneer,
  "Let us see it done here!
What's so oft done with ease, one repeats"

· DEEDS · NOT · WORDS ·

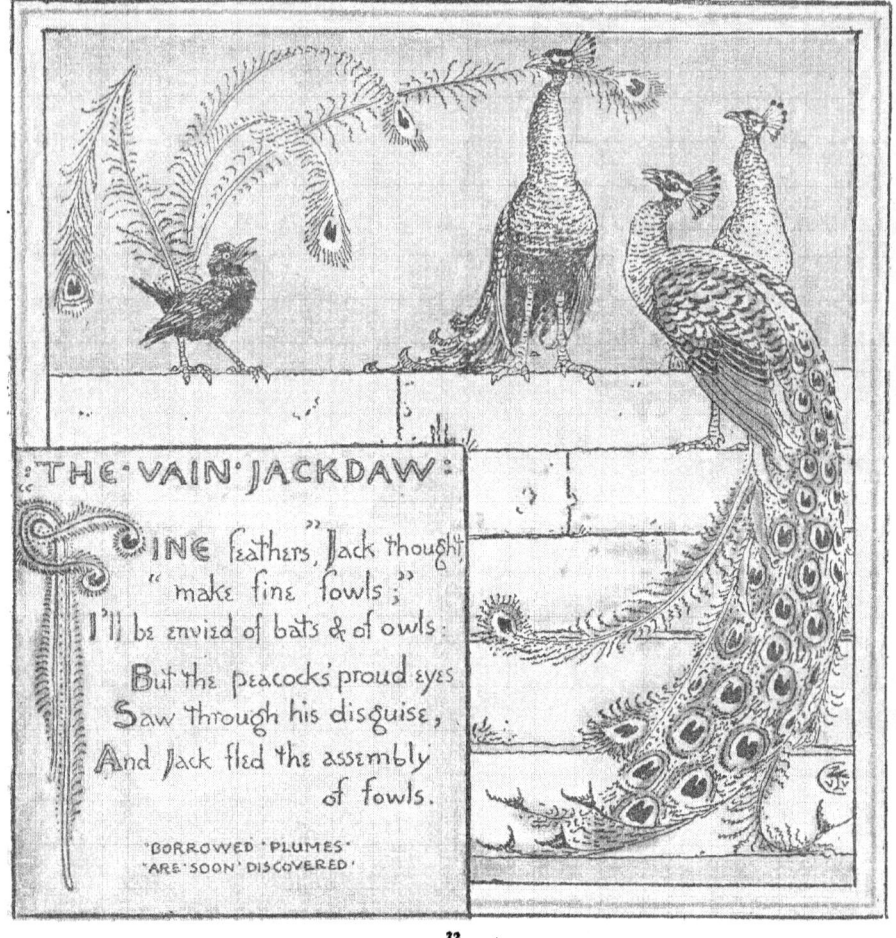

·THE·VAIN·JACKDAW·

"FINE feathers," Jack thought
  "make fine fowls;"
I'll be envied of bats & of owls:
  But the peacocks' proud eyes
  Saw through his disguise,
And Jack fled the assembly
  of fowls.

·BORROWED·PLUMES·
·ARE·SOON·DISCOVERED·

"THE·PEACOCK'S·COMPLAINT"

THE Peacock con-
-sidered it wrong
That he had not the nightingale's
song;
So to Juno he went,
She replied,"Be content
With thy having, & hold thy
fool's tongue!"

"DO·NOT·QUARREL·WITH·NATURE"

33

: THE · TWO · JARS :

NEVER fear! said the Brass
                            to the Clay,
Of two Jars that the flood
                            bore away:
"Keep you close to my side!"
But the porcelain replied,
"I'll be smashed if beside you
                            I stay."

: OUR · FRIEND · OUR · ENEMY :

: THE · TWO · CRABS :

So awkward, so shambling
                            a gait!"
Mrs Crab did her daughter
                            berate,
Who rejoined, "It is true
I am backward; but you
Needed lessons in walking
                            quite late."

: LOOK · AT · HOME :

BROTHER & SISTER

TWIN children: the Girl,
she was plain;
The Brother was handsome &
vain;
"Let him brag of his looks,"
Father said; mind your books!
The best beauty is bred in the brain."

HANDSOME IS AS HANDSOME DOES :

35

THE FOX WITHOUT A TAIL

Said Fox, minus tail in a trap,
"My friends! here's a lucky
    mishap:
Give your tails a short lease!
- But the foxes were n't geese,
And none followed the fashion
        of trap.

: YET · SOME · FASHIONS · HAVE · NO ·
    BETTER · REASON :

36

The DOG & the Shadow.

HIS image the Dog did not
         know,
Or his bone's, in the pond's
         painted show:
" 'T'other dog," so he thought,
  " Has got more than he ought;"
So he snapped, & his dinner
          saw go!

·GREED·IS·SOMETIMES·
        CAUGHT·BY·ITS
  OWN·BAIT

THE CROW & THE PITCHER

How the cunning old
Crow got his drink
When 'twas low in the
pitcher, just think!
Don't say that he spilled it!
With pebbles he filled it,
'Till the water rose up to
the brink.

· USE · YOUR · WITS ·

THE · EAGLE · AND · THE · CROW

The Eagle flew off with a lamb;
Then the Crow thought to lift an old ram,
In his eaglish conceit,
The wool tangled his feet,
And the shepherd laid hold of the sham.

· BEWARE · OF · OVERATING · YOUR · OWN · POWERS ·

·THE·BLIND·DOE·

A poor half-blind Doe her one eye
  kept shoreward, all danger to spy,
    As she fed by the sea,
      Poor innocent! she
  Was shot from a boat passing by.

: WATCH·ON·ALL·SIDES :

THE·GEESE·&·THE·CRANES·

THE Geese joined the Cranes in some wheat;
All was well, till, disturbed at their treat,
Light-winged, the Cranes fled,
But the slow Geese, well fed,
Could n't rise, and were caught in retreat.

BEWARE · OF · ENTERPRIZES · WHERE · THE · RISKS · ARE · NOT · EQUAL ·

THE·TRUMPETER·TAKEN·PRISONER·

A Trumpeter, prisoner made,
Hoped his life would be spared
when he said
He'd no part in the fight,
But they answered him-"Right,
But what of the music you made?"

SONGS·MAY·SERVE
A·CAUSE·AS·WELL·AS·SWORD

: HOT · AND · COLD :

WHEN to warm his cold fingers
man blew,
And again, but to cool the hot stew;
Simple Satyr, unused
To man's ways, felt confused,
When the same mouth blew hot &
cold too!

· ÆSOP · AIMED · AT · DOUBLE · DEALING ·

NEITHER·BEAST·NOR·BIRD·

A Beast he
would be, or
a bird,
As might suit, thought the Bat:
but he erred.
When the battle was done,
He found that no one
Would take him for friend at
his word.

·BETWEEN·TWO·STOOLS·
·YOU·MAY·COME·TO·THE·GROUND·

43

THE·STAG·IN·THE·OX·STALL ❧ THE·DEER·&·THE·LION

SAFE enough lay the poor
              hunted Deer
In the ox-stall, with nothing
                      to fear
From the careless-eyed men :
Till the Master came ; then
There was no hiding-place
        for the Deer.

FROM the hounds the swift
              Deer sped away,
To his cave, where in past times
                          he lay
Well concealed; unaware
Of a Lion couched there,
For a spring that soon made
                  him his prey.

·AN·EYE·IS·
KEEN·IN·ITS
·OWN·
·INTEREST·

·FATE·
·CAN·MEET·
AS·WELL·AS·
·FOLLOW·

44

THE LION IN LOVE

THOUGH the Lion in love let them draw
All his teeth, and pare down every claw,
He'd no bride for his pains,
For they beat out his brains
Ere he set on his maiden a paw.

OUR VERY MEANS MAY DEFEAT OUR ENDS

45

THE · CAT · AND · VENVS

"MIGHT his Cat be a woman", he said:
Venus changed her: the couple were wed:
But a mouse in her sight
Metamorphosed her quite,
And, for bride, a cat found he instead.

: NATURE · WILL · OUT :

MICE · IN · COUNCIL :

AGAINST Cat sat
a Council of Mice.
Every Mouse came out
prompt with advice,
And a bell on Cat's throat
Would have met a round vote,
Had the bell-hanger not
been so nice.

: THE · BEST · POLICY · OFTEN ·
· TURNS · ON · AN · IF :

46

·THE·HEN·AND·THE·FOX·

THE Hen roosted high on her
perch;
Hungry Fox down below, on the
search,
Coaxed her hard to descend
She replied, "Most dear friend !
I feel more secure on my perch "

: BEWARE· OF· INTERESTED· FRIENDSHIPS :

THE·CAT·AND·THE·FOX·

THE Fox said " I can play,
when it fits,
Many wiles that with man make
me quits "
" But my trick's up a tree ! "
Said the Cat, safe to see
Clever Fox hunted out of his wits.

: TRUST· TO· SKILL· RATHER· THAN· WIT :

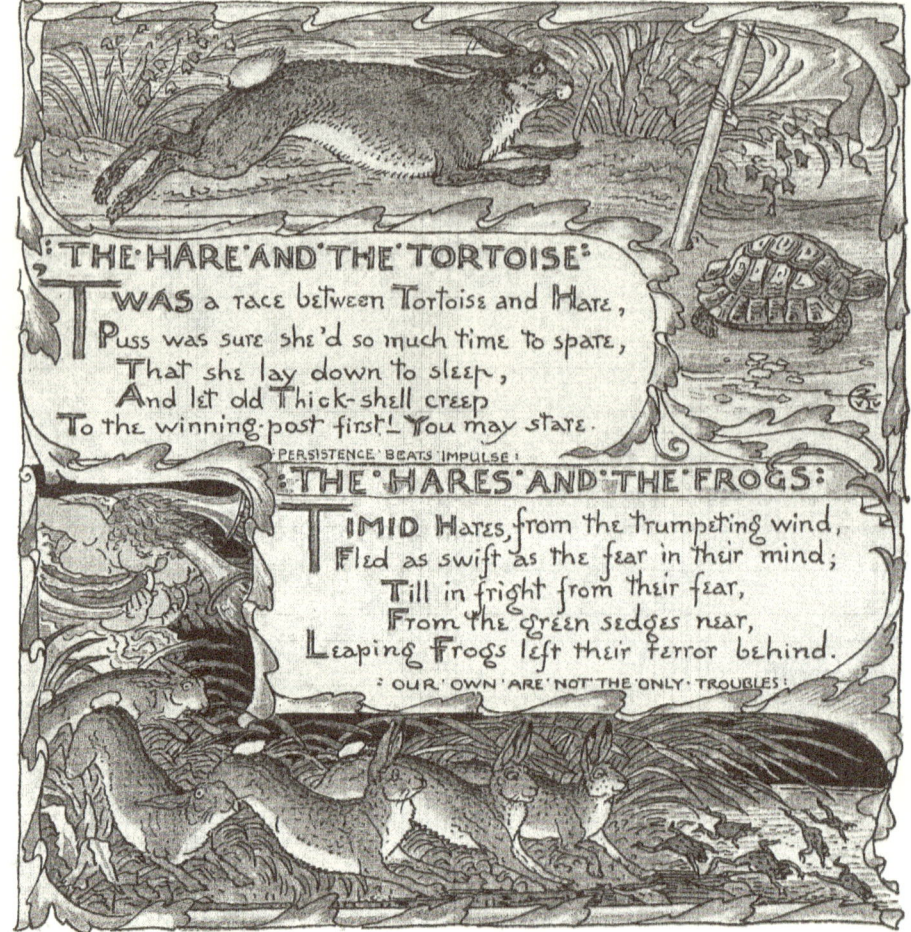

THE·HARE·AND·THE·TORTOISE·

TWAS a race between Tortoise and Hare,
Puss was sure she'd so much time to spare,
   That she lay down to sleep,
   And let old Thick-shell creep
To the winning-post first! You may stare.

·PERSISTENCE·BEATS·IMPULSE·

THE·HARES·AND·THE·FROGS·

TIMID Hares, from the trumpeting wind,
Fled as swift as the fear in their mind;
   Till in fright from their fear,
   From the green sedges near,
Leaping Frogs left their terror behind.

·OUR·OWN·ARE·NOT·THE·ONLY·TROUBLES·

48

PORCUPINE, SNAKE, & COMPANY.

GOING shares with the Snakes, Porcu=
pine
Said "the best of the bargain is mine."
Nor would he back down,
When the snakes would disown
The agreement his quills made them
sign.

· HASTY · PARTNERSHIPS · MAY · BE · REPENTED · OF ·

:THE· BEAR· &·THE·BEES:

THEIR honey I'll have when I
please;
"Who cares for such small things as
Bees?"
Said the Bear; but the stings
Of these very small things
Left him not very much at his ease.

·THE·WEAKEST·UNITED·MAY·BE·STRONG·TO·AVENGE

49

:THE·BUNDLE·OF·STICKS:

To his sons, who fell out, father
                 spake:
"This Bundle of Sticks you can't
               break;"
Take them singly, with ease,
You may break as you please;
So, dissension your strength will
               unmake.

·STRENGTH·IS·IN·UNITY·

THE FARMER'S TREASURE

"DIG deeply, my Sons! through this field!
There's a Treasure — he died:
                        unrevealed
The spot where 'twas laid,
They dug as he bade;
And the Treasure was found in
                        the yield.

PRODUCTIVE LABOUR IS THE ONLY SOURCE OF WEALTH

51

:THE·COCK·THE·ASS·&·THE·LION:

THE Ass gave a horrible bray,
Cock crowed; Lion scampered away;
Ass judged he was scared
By the bray, and so dared
To pursue; Lion ate him they say.

DON'T·TAKE·ALL·THE·CREDIT·TO·YOURSELF·

:THE·ASS·AND·THE·LAP·DOG:

"HOW Master that little Dog pets?"
Thinks the Ass; & with jealousy frets,
So he climbs Master's knees,
Hoping dog-like to please,
And a drubbing is all that he gets.

·ASSES·MUST·NOT·EXPECT·TO·BE·FONDLED·

FORTVNE AND THE BOY

A Boy heedless slept by the well
By Dame Fortune awaked, truth to tell;
Said she, "Hadst been drowned,
'T would have surely been found'
This by Fortune, not Folly befel."

FORTUNE·IS·NOT·ANSWERABLE·FOR·OUR·WANT·OF·FORESIGHT·

THE·UNGRATEFUL·WOLF·

TO the Wolf, from whose throat
           D.r Crane
Drew the bone, his long bill made
           it plain
   He expected his fee:
    Snarled Wolf—"Fiddle de dee,
Be thankful your head's out again"

·SOME·CHARACTERS·
·HAVE·NO·SENSE·OF·OBLIGATION·

·THE·FISHERMAN·&·THE·FISH·

PRAYED the Fish, as the Fisherman took
  Him, a poor little mite, from his hook,
    "Let me go! I'm so small."
    He replied, "Not at all!
You're the biggest, perhaps in the brook."

·A·LITTLE·CERTAINTY·IS·BETTER·THAN·A·GREAT·CHANCE·

THE·HERDSMANS·VOWS

A KID vowed to Jove, so might he
Find his herd, & his herd did he see
Soon, of lions the prey:
Then 'twas - "Get me away,
And a goat of the best take for fee.,,

:HOW·OFTEN·WOULD·WE·MEND·OUR·WISHES !

THE·HORSE·AND·THE·ASS:

O VERLADEN the Ass was. The Horse
Would n't help; but had time for remorse
When the Ass lay dead there;
For he then had to bear
Both the load of the Ass & his corse.

GRUDGE·NOT·HELP !

THE·ASS·&·THE·SICK·LION:

CRAFTY Lion,—perhaps with the gout
Kept his cave; where, to solve any doubt,
    Many visitors go:
    But the Ass, he said "No!
They go in, but I've seen none come out."
·REASON·FROM·RESULTS·

·THE·END·

www.ingramcontent.com/pod-product-compliance
Lightning Source LLC
Chambersburg PA
CBHW022157020726
47496CB00008B/2760